Thomasina
and the
Tommyknocker

allison B.

THOMASINA
and the
TOMMYKNOCKER

Juanita Kennedy Browne

Illustrated by Allison Bridgman

BROWNE BOOKS IN THE HOLLOW

Published by Browne Books in The Hollow
11252 Zorita Court, San Diego, CA 92124

Designed and produced by Dave Comstock
Printed on acid-free recycled paper by Thomson-Shore Inc.

Other books by the same author
(Published by The Nevada County Historical Society):

Nuggets of Nevada County History

*A Tale of Two Cities and a Train: History of the
Nevada County Narrow Gauge Railroad*

Sketches of Yesterday and Today in Nevada County
(Illustrated by Marilyn Starkey)

Library of Congress Cataloging-in-Publication Data

Browne, Juanita Kennedy, 1929–1993
Thomasina and the Tommyknocker / Juanita Kennedy Browne ;
illustrated by Allison Bridgman.
p. cm.
Includes bibliographical references.
Summary: A young girl in a California gold mining town in 1892 meets a
mythical Cornish creature associated with underground mines and learns a
lesson about what it takes to become someone who is truly important.
ISBN 0-9636621-0-4
[1. Conduct of life—Fiction. 2. Gold mines and mining—Fiction.
3. California—Fiction.] I. Bridgman, Allison, ill. II. Title.
III. Title: Thomasina and the Tommyknocker.
PZ7.B82214Th 1993
[Fic]—dc20   93-13732
CIP
AC

This

book is dedicated

to everyone who ever

wanted to Be Somebody

and found they already were; to

my grandchildren, Allison and Joe,

who were my inspiration; to parents,

grandparents, relatives, families, friends,

historians, and teachers who want to share a

part of their history with the young and young at heart,

to the child who lives on in me,

and

AS ALWAYS,

TO PETE

My Thanks

To Marilyn, Penny, Pamela, Margaret, Ruth, Willa, Joe, Allison, Kathy Jo, Dave, Karen, Julee, Joan, Madelyn, and everyone who gave me encouragement and advice—even those who were my harshest critics and told me there were no female Tommyknockers.

My special thanks to the students at Ready Springs Union Elementary School, who gave me encouragement when I needed it most.

JUANITA KENNEDY BROWNE

About Tommyknockers

According to popular Cornish legend, Tommyknockers are tiny male miners who live deep underground in hard-rock mines. They tap on timbers and rocks to warn their fellow miners when there is danger of cave-ins, floods, falling rocks, or deadly gases. Human miners have learned to listen for the tap, tap, tap of the Tommyknockers so they, too, can escape from danger.

Tommyknockers are easily insulted and quick to anger, especially by people who do not believe in Tommyknockers and the magic of the imagination and Christmas.

Contrary to popular belief, there are also female Tommyknockers. On rare occasions they will warn a special person of danger.

This is the story of a special young girl and her brief meeting with a female Tommyknocker.

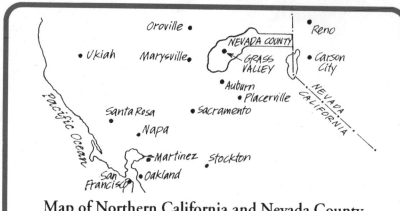

Map of Northern California and Nevada County.

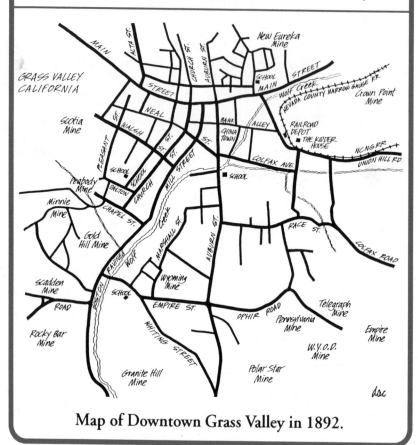

Map of Downtown Grass Valley in 1892.

Chapter 1

Grass Valley, California, December 12, 1892, 10:30 a.m. The shriek of the whistle of the little "Never Come, Never Go" train engine pierced through the pounding rain. Ten-year-old Thomasina Starr squirmed in her seat.

Aching anteater, Thomasina thought. How I wish I could be at the depot to meet Brother Pete when he comes in on the train next Monday. But I'll be stuck in this old classroom.

Thomasina sighed.

The little "Never Come, Never Go" train heads for Grass Valley.

The room was stuffy with smells of warm bodies, wet wool, wood smoke, chalk dust, and sweat on wooden desks.

Next to the roaring pot-bellied stove, Miss Fanny Doom droned on about plans for Donation Day.

Thomasina blew back a string of hair from her dark brown eyes. She scratched her skinny leg and tugged up her gray woolen stocking

Thomasina's mind wandered. It will be good to have Brother Pete home for two weeks. Has college changed him? Will he be too grown-up to play our crazy critters game?

Thomasina's head suddenly snapped back. Joe, who sat behind her, jerked again at a strand of her stringy black hair.

The room was stuffy with the smells of warm bodies.

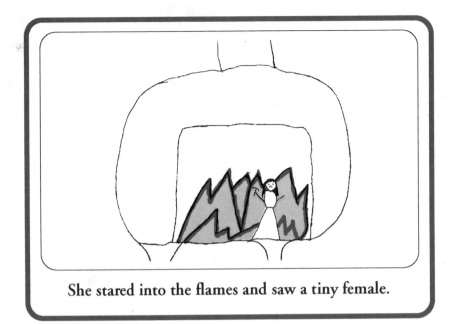

She stared into the flames and saw a tiny female.

"Barking butterflies," Thomasina mumbled as she twisted angrily in her seat and glared at Joe.

· Joe crossed his eyes and warned, "Better pay attention, Tom, Tom. Miss Doom has her big glass eyes on you."

Thomasina hissed, "Joe, the bigger you get, the dumber you get. Snot-nosed snakes. Wipe your drippy nose." She smirked as Joe's freckled face flamed red.

Joe swiped at his nose with his shirt sleeve.

Thomasina screwed up her face and said, "Yuck!"

The room fell silent. The tick, tick, tick of the large classroom clock and the splash-dash of the rain on the wooden roof boomed in Thomasina's ears. As she stared into the flames in the pot-bellied stove, she saw a strangely dressed tiny female figure.

3

Must be what Mother Kate calls a figment of my wild imagination, Thomasina thought. She looks like a female Tommyknocker. But she can't be. Everyone knows that Tommyknockers are males and they are rarely seen or heard outside of the mines. Or are they?

Crack! Miss Doom smacked her ruler against the stove..

Thomasina jumped and looked up. Miss Doom stood tall and silent. She stared down her long, thin nose directly at Thomasina and Joe.

Miss Doom cleared her throat and pushed at her round, thick eyeglasses. She said in a solemn, pay-attention tone, "Students, I would appreciate having your **full** attention. As you know there are some families in our area who do not have as much as others. This is unfortunate, but not unusual for small gold mining towns such as ours.

"Some of the mines have shut down for the winter. Several families are without wood and food."

Miss Doom drew a deep breath, walked around the stove, glanced at each of her 12 pupils, and continued. "To make matters worse, many miners have been injured in mining accidents. Some have been killed. Their families are without a male wage-earner. Thomasina and Joe should be well aware of this."

Thomasina felt a ton of rocks drop on her. She could hardly breathe. It was three years ago. She would **never** forget the screech, screech, screech of the mine whistle. She was in school when she heard it. Everyone knew what it meant. Accident! Help!

Thomasina and her friends with their fathers, uncles, and brothers who worked underground in the Grass Valley gold mines.

Her father, Thomas Starr, was the supervisor of the Polar Starr mine. He heard the whistle and dashed to help dig out four miners who were trapped in the cave-in. As the miners were carried from the shaft, a huge boulder loosened by the cave-in fell and killed Thomas Starr.

Thomasina tried to swallow around a tight lump in her throat.

Where were the Tommyknockers then? Thomasina thought bitterly. They should have warned father that the rock was going to fall so he could have gotten out of the way. But they didn't.

The lump in her throat grew larger. Thomasina clenched her fists and drew a shaky breath. Why did old Miss Gloom and Doom have to remind me? Why did Father have to die?

Thomasina knew that her family was not the only family with troubles. Joe's father was out of work. A few weeks ago, a runaway ore car hurled down the mine shaft, hit him, and crushed his leg. Thomasina felt sorry for Joe. But her own troubles hurt more. Thomasina's father had always made her feel special. Now, at times, Thomasina felt lost and unimportant.

It just isn't fair, she thought.

Hot, angry tears stabbed at Thomasina's eyes. She held

Boys carried gifts of firewood on Donation Day.

them back. She tossed her hair, stiffened her back, and stared at Miss Doom with defiance.

Miss Doom shifted her gaze and finished her lecture. "Class, Donation Day will be held on Friday, the sixteenth of December. Everyone who can shall bring a stick of wood, a potato, canned goods, or discarded garments to class that day. As you know, these donations will be given to needy families by the Ladies Relief Society. Even one small potato will help."

Miss Doom added, "Of course, the boys will march in the parade that will begin at the railroad depot. Girls may watch the parade from the wooden sidewalks and then bring their donations to class."

Thomasina knew the story of Donation Day. She had watched the men and boys march in the annual parades since she was four years old. Her father had taken up donations at the Polar Starr mine because the miners didn't get off to watch the parade. He told her that although the miners made only $3 a day, they dug deep into their pockets and gave what they could to help others.

He had told her many times how the tradition of Donation Day began. Winters had always been hard on the mining community. One December, an invalid lady had an idea as she watched children pass her window on their way to school. She wrote a letter to the editor of *The Union* news-paper. She suggested that each child from all the different schools bring one stick of wood or one potato to school to help the needy. That was the way Donation Day began.

As these thoughts rushed through Thomasina's mind she

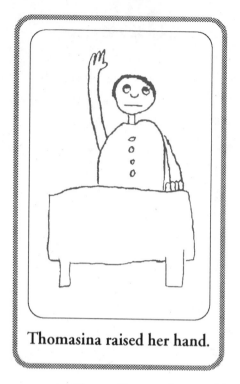

Thomasina raised her hand.

bumped into a question. Thomasina threw up her hand and blurted, "Why? Why can't girls march in the parade?"

Miss Doom looked down her long, thin nose and pulled her body into a long, thin line. She said through tight lips, "Thomasina, when will you learn to hold your tongue? You were not given permission to speak. Your behavior is most unladylike."

Thomasina dropped her head and mumbled, "I'm sorry."

She really wasn't. *Freckled foxes,* she thought. I hate being told I should be seen, not heard. I don't want to be a lady. All they do is sit around in piles of petticoats and long, stiff dresses with stupid smiles on their faces.

Miss Doom let her disapproving silence seep around the room.

Thomasina **had** to know. She lifted her head, pushed a wisp of hair from her eyes, and raised her hand slowly.

Miss Doom ignored her. The large school clock tick, tocked. The rain hammered at the roof and windows. The wood fire crackled. Outside, the stamp mills boom, boomed, boomed. The train whistle screeched

8

Thomasina glanced at her red-haired friend, Colleen Steel. Colleen rolled her eyes back and mouthed the word, "Trouble!"

Thomasina turned to re-face Miss Doom. Several girls giggled. Thomasina swiveled and gave them a long, dirty look. Joe whispered, "The fastest mouth in the West shoots from the hip again."

Thomasina gritted her teeth. *Gartered 'gators,* she thought. What does a big red-headed woodpecker with a drippy nose know anyway? She shuffled her feet and jerked at her saggy stockings with one hand. She kept the other hand raised. She waited.

The clock tick, tocked. The stamp mills boom, boomed. Thomasina's heart thudded. Finally, Miss Doom sighed and said, "Yes, Thomasina?"

Thomasina blurted, "Miss Doom, please, why can't girls march in the parade? After all Donation Day was a lady's idea."

Miss Doom tap, tapped her ruler on the stove and said with each beat. "Yes *(tap)*, Donation Day *(tap)* was a

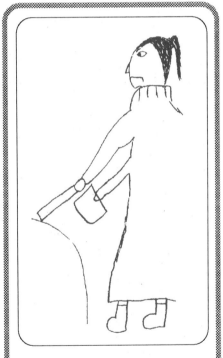

Miss Doom tap, tapped her ruler on the potbelly stove.

9

lady's idea *(tap)*. But the parade was *not (SMACK!)*. The parade was started by boys and male merchants. Ladies and girls do *not (SMACK!)* march in the parade. It has **never** been done."

Thomasina jumped to her feet and blurted, "Is there a law against it?"

Miss Doom, somewhat startled, replied, "No, No, of course not. There is no law against girls marching in the Donation Day parade. It is simply **not done!** That is the end of this discussion, Miss Thomasina Starr. Be seated and be silent."

Thomasina flopped into her seat and blew a wisp of hair from her eyes.

Joe whispered, "Guess that puts you in your place, Little Miss Big Mouth. You make more noise than a stamp mill."

Thomasina ignored Joe's jabs. She knew he was just teasing her. He did it all the time. He was like a big puppy yapping at a small kitten. He wanted Thomasina to spit back and bare her claws.

Thomasina didn't care much for boys. But she liked Joe—a little. She knew Joe wasn't really dumb. Mother Kate called Joe "an unpolished gold nugget." Mother Kate said that as Joe grew up and rubbed against the world, he would shine. Thomasina doubted it.

As Thomasina slumped sullenly in her seat, she stared into the fire. She saw the tiny figure again. She was marching around in the flames waving a tiny miner's pick like a baton.

Miss Doom's words echoed in Thomasina's mind. "It has **never** been done." An idea began to hammer inside Thomasina's head.

10

Thomasina squirmed in her seat, motioned to Colleen, and pointed to the figure in the fire. Colleen looked in the direction of Thomasina's pointed finger. She looked back at Thomasina, raised her eyebrows, and shrugged her shoulders.

Thomasina looked into the flames again. The figure was gone.

By the time Colleen looked in the direction of Thomasina's pointed finger, the tiny female figure had vanished.

Chapter 2

When class was dismissed, Thomasina and Colleen rushed into the cloak room. As Thomasina jerked her coat from its hanger, Rowdy, the class bully, skidded in and slammed Thomasina against the wall.

"Weeping warthogs," Thomasina yelled. "Why did you do that you big dumb ox?"

Rowdy snarled, "Well, if it isn't Miss Fast Mouth who thinks girls should march in the Donation Parade. I'm warning you, just don't . . ."

Colleen swirled and punched Rowdy in the stomach with a handful of books.

"Ooff!" Rowdy bent double and grabbed his stomach.

Before Rowdy could catch his breath, Colleen grabbed Thomasina's hand. They dashed through the cloak room and outside. The rain had turned into a gentle mist.

They ran to catch up with Joe and a group of their class mates. They knew Rowdy was too big a coward to bother them with Joe around.

As they fell in with the group, Thomasina gasped, "Thanks, Colleen. You really gave Rowdy a biff in his belly."

Colleen shrugged her shoulders and said, "We poor help-less girls gotta' stick up for each other."

Thomasina and her classmates in front of the schoolhouse.

Joe laughed and said, "I'd say you both do a good job of that."

Colleen turned to Thomasina and asked, "What was all that pointing at the stove about?"

Thomasina pulled Colleen aside and whispered, "Do you believe in female Tommyknockers?"

Colleen rolled her dark green eyes and shook her fiery hair that had frizzed tight from the mist. "Faith and be-gor-ra," she said in a fake Irish accent. "Did Rowdy hit you harder than I thought? Now, and sure, who ever heard of a fee-male Tommy-knocker? Let me feel your noggin'. Have you a fever, girl?"

Thomasina angrily knocked Colleen's hand away.

"Oh, come now, Thomasina. As a true Irish colleen if I

13

were seeing the little people, they would be leprechauns, not Tommyknockers. Why? Do you *think* you saw a Tommyknocker?"

Thomasina shook her head and mumbled, "Of course not. I was just wondering . . . ." She bit her tongue and looked away. "Well, guess we won't be playing any softball in this rain, will we?"

Colleen's green eyes narrowed as she looked at Thomasina closely. "Are you sure you're . . ."

Some schools were so small that one teacher taught boys and girls of different ages and grades in a single room.

Thomasina glared at Colleen.

Colleen looked away and changed the subject. "It's probably just as well. Our old softball is about to fall apart anyway. It can't last much longer."

When they parted at Mill street, Colleen waved and yelled, "Watch out for Rowdy. He can cause more trouble than any male **or** female Tommyknocker."

Thomasina grabbed her back, faked a limp, and yelled back, "Yeah, I can feel it in my bones. All the ones he tried to break."

Chapter 3

As she walked on home, Thomasina kicked rocks and fallen pine cones. The feeling of being small and unimportant clouded her mind.

Thomasina loved her little world. The small gold mining town of Grass Valley was the only world she knew. But she wanted to feel special again like her father always made her feel. She wanted to **Be Somebody**. Somebody other than "Pete's little sister" or "the Widow Starr's little girl."

She wanted to do something that would make people look up to her and admire her.

As much as Thomasina loved her mother and brother, she wanted to be known for something she did all by herself.

Local people had great respect for her mother. Mother Kate was a talented artist. Her drawings of local people and places were published in several New York magazines. Thomasina thought the drawings were nice, but she didn't understand the big hullabaloo they caused in New York.

Mother Kate was well paid for her drawings. That's how they had gotten by since Thomas Starr's death. Thomasina had heard that Easterners couldn't see enough of the strange people and places in the Wild West of California.

Waltzing whales, Thomasina thought. Wild West, indeed.

The people in Mother's drawings are just ordinary people like Ah Ling, Chief Wema, Juan Juarez, Irish Tim, and Cornish Lou. I don't see anything wild or special about them. And what's so special about gold mines? There are hundreds of them around here?

Thomasina kicked another pine cone and mulled over her problem.

She smiled as she thought of Brother Pete. Everyone liked Pete. He was a good student and a hard worker. Before he got a scholarship to go to college, he worked after school for the local newspaper. He was good at all kinds of sports and wrote articles about horse races at Glenbrook Park, Cornish wrestling matches at Grass Valley, and local football and baseball games.

He taught Thomasina and Colleen how to play softball. Sometimes Pete and Joe would let the girls join in a game when Rowdy wasn't around. Rowdy thought girls didn't belong on earth, let alone in a softball game.

The boys liked Pete. The girls giggled when he came around. Thomasina didn't like that.

Thomasina loved her family. But she longed to Be Somebody. How could she do it?

Purple porcupines. **Was** that a female Tommyknocker I saw in the stove? Why was she marching around with a miner's pick? What was she trying to tell me?

Suddenly, Thomasina was smacked over the head with a great idea. "Long-eared lizards," she shouted to the gloomy sky. "The Donation Day parade is my chance. If I march, people will look up to me as 'Thomasina, the first girl to march.' I'll get my name in the paper! I'll be famous."

Thomasina tossed her hair back and began to quick-march home. She would do it.

As Thomasina marched past the old abandoned mine shaft near her home, she heard a tap, tap, tap. She ignored the sound. She thought it was just another prospector pounding away at rocks and looking for gold.

Suddenly, the image of the tiny female flashed into Thomasina's mind. Maybe, just maybe, the tapping **is** a female Tommyknocker trying to warn me of something. But what? Or who? The parade? Rowdy?

Thomasina shook her head and mumbled, "Wake up, girl." Maybe Rowdy did scramble my brains. But I'll just show him!

Hardrock gold miners with their Cornish lunch pails.

Chapter 4

As Thomasina banged through the front door of the cabin, Zeke barked and ran to greet her. Thomasina patted his big head and smiled. Everyone smiled at Zeke. He was a large, shaggy, black and white English setter. One eye was darkened by a big black patch. Zeke looked like a doggie pirate, and he stole people's hearts with his clumsy friendliness.

Thomasina yelled, "I'm home."

Mother Kate called, "So I hear. I'm back here, my merry girl."

Thomasina threw her lunch pail on the kitchen table and pinched off a corner of a fresh-baked cobbler. She jammed the piece in her mouth as she and Zeke barged through the door to the little room her mother called her studio.

"Hello, Mother. Have a good day drawing?"

"Yes, yes, I did. And as soon as you have a slice of peach cobbler and a glass of Old Betsy's milk, I would like you to deliver some drawings to our friends."

Thomasina loved her mother's studio. It smelled of ink and summer. Bunches of dried flowers and herbs hung from the ceiling. The walls were covered with a curious collection. Mother Kate's studio was like a small showcase of the people and cultures of Grass Valley.

Kate would make several drawings before she sent the final one to her New York publisher. She would hang one in her studio. Then, each Christmas, she gave a drawing to everyone who had posed for her during the year. In return, they often gave her a handmade Christmas gift. Mother Kate treasured these unusual gifts. She hung them on the studio walls with her drawings.

Kate often told Thomasina that a handmade gift that came from the imagination and the heart was more precious than gold.

As Thomasina wandered around the room she touched some of the gifts. These are pretty, she thought, but I would rather have the gold.

Thomasina studied a tiny Indian basket that Chief Wema's wife had given Kate last year. The basket, woven from native plants, was a miniature of the baskets the Indian women used when they gathered acorn nuts in the fall.

Thomasina asked, "Who's your latest model?"

Kate held up a drawing.

"No doubt about that face," Thomasina said. "It's Old Zeb the liveryman. Looks so real I can almost hear him say . . ."

"Yeap, you bet!" they said together and laughed.

Another idea popped up. Old Zeb was just the man Thomasina wanted to see.

After gulping down her cobbler and milk, Thomasina called Zeke. They crashed out the door with Kate's drawings in a large basket.

As they dashed from place to place and delivered Mother

Kate's drawings, Thomasina was given special handmade gifts to take to her mother.

An apple doll from the German hotelkeeper, Mrs. Sonntag.

A wooden Hawaiian angel from Kemo Hanu, a Hawaiian miner who boarded with the widow Jones.

A cornhusk doll with a black face from Lisa Shank, the cook at the Gold Hill boarding house. Everyone knew the story of Lisa, who had worked to buy her husband out of slavery before the Civil War.

A purple paper origami bird from Kato, the Japanese vegetable vendor.

Ah Ling, the Chinese laundryman, had painted a large egg with Chinese good luck symbols.

Miss Wren, the small, timid seamstress gave a package of colorful snippets of ribbons and lace.

Miss Cornish Lou hugged Thomasina to her large powdered bosom and gave her an ostrich plume dyed bright red. "Imported at great expense from the new ostrich farm in Southern California," she boomed in Thomasina's ear.

Juan Juarez, the Mexican mule skinner, shyly handed Thomasina a small donkey-shaped piñata. "For the señora and señorita," he said with a slight bow.

Thomasina placed each gift carefully in her big basket and gave each person a sincere but hurried "Thank You, Thank You." She and Zeke then rushed to their next stop.

Their last stop was Old Zeb's livery stable and saddlery.

Thomasina handed Old Zeb her mother's drawing and said, "Merry Christmas to you from Mother."

Zeb rubbed his long beard, puffed on his pipe, slowly nodded his head, and said, "Yeap. You bet."

Dimpled dragons, Thomasina thought. He likes it. Now's the time to ask.

Thomasina blurted, "Can you make saddlebags so Zeke can carry some jars and sticks of wood like a pack mule?"

Zeb gave Zeke a long look.

Thomasina quickly added, "I can't pay you. But I can run errands for you and help feed the horses and clean out the stalls after school."

Old Zeb said, "Yeap, you bet. Come back Wednesday."

After school on Wednesday, Thomasina and Zeke barreled through the stable door. Thomasina yelled into the darkness, "Hey, Zeb, are Zeke's saddlebags ready?"

Old Zeb came out of the shadows and handed her the small saddlebags. A row of sleigh bells jingled.

Thomasina said, "Dancing donkeys. It's perfect. Zeke can easily carry some jars and wood in this. And he can march to his own music."

Old Zeb's eyes sparkled. He showed Thomasina how to strap the saddlebags onto Zeke. Zeb said, "When you load him, put equal weights on each side.

"Mrs. Kate's drawing of me is nice. No charge. My gift. My pleasure. Yeap. You bet."

That was the longest speech Thomasina had ever heard from Old Zeb.

"Bow-tied bears," Thomasina shouted. She smiled her best smile and said, "Thank you, thank you. This is wonderful."

Old Zeb nodded and said, "Yeap. You bet."

"Put equal weights on both sides," said Old Zeb.

As Thomasina skipped home, she threw back her head and shouted to the rapidly changing cloud formations, "We're going to march."

In one fluffy cloud, the tiny female figure formed. The figure pounded on a rock with a tiny miner's pick. Her gray hair was long and stringy, and her face changed rapidly from smiles to frowns.

Mother Kate had taught Thomasina to look for shapes and figures in clouds and in the bark on trees and in the rain stains on the ceiling of her room. Kate said it was good exercise. It would keep Thomasina's imagination from getting lazy. Mother Kate claimed a strong imagination had magical powers.

"Toe-tapping Tommyknockers," Thomasina said to the figure in the cloud. "What are you and what are you trying to tell me?"

Thomasina stooped to pat Zeke's big head and asked, "What do you think, Zeke? Could there really be female Tommyknockers? Joe and Rowdy would sure get a big laugh if I told them what I've seen lately. Even Colleen thinks I've got rocks in my head."

Zeke wagged his big tail and smiled his big smile. Thomasina touched his silky ears to her cheeks and sniffed his doggy smell. She said, "Come on, Zeke, let's run. It's getting late."

With his head held high and his feathery tail blowing in the breeze, Zeke jingled after her.

During the next few days, Thomasina packed and re-packed the saddlebags and marched Zeke around her bed-room. The sleigh bells tinkled merrily. With practice, Thomasina learned how much weight to put on each side so the saddlebags wouldn't slip sideways. Zeke seemed happy with the whole affair.

Chapter 5

On Donation Day, Thomasina awakened to the sounds and smells she knew so well. The loud pound, pound, pound of the large metal stamp mills was as familiar as the soft thump of her heart. She paid little attention to either. The stamp mills and her heart pounded twenty-four hours a day, every day of the week.

Thomasina stretched her toes into a cold spot between the sheets and shivered under her warm, fluffy comforter. The bright sun crashed through her window and sparkled on the photograph of her father on her dresser. Thomasina said, "Good morning, Father. We miss you and love you."

As she squinted into the sparkling sunlight, the tiny female figure danced across the top of her father's photograph. Thomasina asked the image, "Who are you? Why do I see you?"

As if in answer, Old Betsy mooed loudly for her morning milking. Thomasina turned her head slightly and the image vanished.

From behind the house she heard the chop, chop, chop of Pete splitting wood for the cook stove. It was good to have him home from college for the holidays.

The clang of pots on the iron stove echoed from the

kitchen. Thomasina's nose twitched at the mixed smells of fried bacon and gingerbread cookies.

Mother Kate called from the kitchen. "Hurry up, Thomasina, we've aplenty to do today. Breakfast is ready, and these cookies need to be wrapped for Donation Day. Be up and about, my merry girl."

Thomasina thought, Mother Kate, you have no idea of how much aplenty I have to do today.

Zeke nosed open the bedroom door and padded to the

The large metal stamp mills pounded 24 hours a day.

side of Thomasina's bed. As he nudged her face with his cold nose, Thomasina breathed in his warm doggy breath and said, "Laughing llamas. Today you and I will make history. By the time the newspaper hits the streets tomorrow afternoon, we'll be famous."

Zeke wagged his large tail and smiled. Zeke seemed to approve. Zeke seemed to approve of just about everything, including kids and kittens.

Thomasina whispered her secret wish into Zeke's floppy

ears, "I love my family, Zeke, but I want people to see **me**. I want to do something to get people's attention. That's why I'm marching."

Pete's voice boomed from the kitchen, "Spitting spiders. Come on sister sleepy-head. Out of bed. The sun isn't waiting on you. So be up and about."

Thomasina giggled. It was good to hear Pete play their crazy critters game. College wasn't taking all the fun out of him.

She sang back, "Tap-dancing tigers. I'm up and at 'em." Thomasina dressed in her warmest clothes and tugged on an old pair of work boots. Although the sun was up, the air was cold. The big, bare walnut tree outside her window sparkled with frost diamonds. This time of year a rainstorm could move in quickly. She wasn't going to let a little rain stop **her** parade.

After she was dressed, Thomasina stooped and pulled out Zeke's saddlebags from under her bed. The bags were loaded with four sticks of wood, two on each side, and four jars of peaches, two on each side.

Thomasina had helped her mother can the peaches from their tiny orchard last summer. Thomasina had chopped the wood from a small fallen oak.

She told Zeke, "If gifts from the hands are as good as gold, like Mother says, these should be worth a whole poke full of gold."

Mother Kate and Thomasina had also wrapped some of Thomas Starr's warmest work clothes into a small, colorful bundle. They had agreed the clothes would do more good warming someone in need than hanging unused in the closet.

Thomasina decided she would march with that precious bundle. She would also carry Mother Kate's fresh baked cookies so they wouldn't get crushed in Zeke's pack.

Thomasina said with pride, "Zeke, you look as happy as a decorated dormouse. Let's go show Mother and Pete."

Zeke and Thomasina banged through the kitchen door and marched around the kitchen. Zeke's bells jingled.

Pete said, "Belled bats. What have we here?"

Thomasina proudly announced, "What we have here are marchers in the Donation Day parade. And, I wish to add, the

first female marcher and her do-gooder dog, Zeke."

Mother Kate banged a too-hot plate of biscuits onto the table. She said simply, "That's nice."

Pete said, "Do tell?"

Thomasina's face fell. She blurted, "Don't you know what a great idea this is? Old Zeb made Zeke's saddlebags. But the idea is all **mine**."

The first female marcher and her do-gooder dog, Zeke.

Pete rolled his eyes and shook his head. "Glowing garter snakes and shades of Susan B. Anthony. Don't tell me we have a suffragette in our midst!"

Thomasina was puzzled. She didn't like the sound of that. She didn't want to suffer. She wanted to march and have fun

29

and Be Somebody. She asked, "What's a suffragette?"

Mother Kate smiled and said, "Sit down and eat your breakfast or you'll be late. We need to wrap the gingerbread cookies."

Thomasina plopped down in her seat and angrily jammed food into her mouth. She couldn't believe they didn't understand how important this was to her.

Pete ignored her angry pout and explained, "A suffragette is a woman who wants the right to vote—just like men. Black males got the right to vote with the passage of the Fifteenth Amendment to the Constitution. Women—black or white—didn't. Wyoming is the only state that allows women to vote in local elections. Suffragettes have staged marches to get attention. Some of them have been jailed."

Thomasina squirmed in her seat. *Pea-brained peacocks,* she thought. Maybe Pete **was** getting stuffed with too many book facts. Thomasina didn't want a stupid history lesson. But she didn't like this. What if Miss Doom was wrong? What if it **was** against the law for females to march in the Donation Day parade? What if the marshal threw her in the calaboose? *Queasy quails.* Do I dare march?

Pete saw Thomasina squirm. He leaned closer and said in a solemn whisper, "When the suffragettes went on a hunger strike and refused to eat, the jailers stuck long tubes down their throats and dumped cold, lumpy oatmeal into their bellies."

Thomasina felt the blood drain from her face. She shuddered and said, "Yuck!"

Mother Kate said, "Pete, that's enough. The point is this.

Why do you want to march, Thomasina?"

For once, Thomasina was at a loss for words. She didn't want to say that she was tired of being called "Pete's little sister" or "the Widow Starr's little girl." She loved them. But she did so want to Be Somebody. On her own.

Thomasina twisted a strand of her black hair, bit her lip, and thought hard. "Well, uh, uh . . ."

Pete crowed. "Gargling gorillas. Don't you know **why**?"

Thomasina's mind raced. She knew what Donation Day was all about. She grabbed at a passing thought. "Of course, I know, you crowing centipede. I want to march to help the needy. Miss Doom says it's not against the law. I don't think the needy care if a boy or girl carries the donations."

As her mind charged full steam ahead, her words tumbled out. "I don't think the needy care if girls walk down the wooden walks to keep their shoes clean or tromp through the muddy streets. Just so they deliver the donations. I'm not afraid of getting mud on my boots."

Mother Kate smiled her dreamy smile, and said, "If that's the reason you want to march, I see no harm in it. It **is** your choice."

Pete shook his head in disbelief. "Jumping June bugs. She's going to become a female crusader like Allison Coleman."

Thomasina frowned. She didn't like Allison. Allison Coleman and Beatrice Kidder were friends. They went to a private school. They had curly hair and wore pretty dresses and big bows in their hair. Beatrice was the adopted daughter of rich Mr. Kidder who owned the local railroad. Allison's father was a rich mine owner. They both got everything they wanted.

To make matters worse, Allison was smart. She had won all kinds of speech and essay contests. She was always writing letters to *The Union* newspaper telling everyone what was wrong with everything. Worse than that, Pete got all cow-eyed whenever he looked at Allison. Thomasina definitely didn't like that.

Daffy dinosaurs. My fast mouth has done it again. I **have** to march or they'll think I'm a ninny.

The Never Come, Never Go engine blew a long, shrill blast.

Chapter 6

With the package of cookies tucked under one arm and the bundle of clothes under the other, Thomasina trudged toward town. Zeke jingled along beside her.

Thomasina was worried. Getting to Be Somebody was not going to be as easy as she thought.

As she passed the old mine shaft, she heard a loud tap, tap, tap. Zeke whined softly. Thomasina grabbed Zeke by the collar and said, "Come on, Zeke, we've got to hurry. We don't want to be late for our big day. . . . If it **will** be to be our big day."

Clouds gathered in the sky and in Thomasina's mind. Do I dare go through with this? Is a Tommyknocker trying to warn me against marching in the parade? Maybe Rowdy **will** try to break every bone in my body.

A few blocks away, the Never Come, Never Go engine blew a long, shrill blast. Its bell clang, clanged calling the marchers to gather at the railroad depot.

As Thomasina turned the corner onto Auburn Street, she saw the wagon load of wood that John Kidder donated each year. In front of the wagon pulled by a team of horses, a group of boys scuffled. Some had slung big sticks of wood over their shoulders. Others had potatoes hanging from strings looped around their necks. Some swung their potatoes at each other.

Thomasina spied Joe. He had one of the biggest pieces of wood. Just like Jughead Joe, she thought. She stopped short. Rowdy was with him.

Zeroed zebras. I'm in for it now!

When Rowdy spied Thomasina and Zeke, he yelled, "Hey, Big Mouth. What's that stupid thing on your stupid dog?"

Thomasina clinched her fists. She yelled back, "You should be as smart as Zeke. You ignoramus."

Rowdy didn't know what ignoramus meant, but he knew it wasn't good. He yelled, "Well, Miss Know-it-all, what do you think you and that stupid dog are doing?"

Thomasina shouted, "We're marching."

Rowdy threw back his head and gave a loud, mean laugh. "Not in this parade. Run along and join the girls on the sidewalk where you belong."

Thomasina turned and glanced at a group of girls huddled on the walkway. *Galloping Gnats.* It was Allison and Beatrice and the older girls from their private school.

They were all dressed alike. Their curled hairdos were topped with large blue bows that matched their blue and white uniforms. Their high-buttoned black boots were shiny and new.

They drew into a tighter circle, looked back at Thomasina, and giggled. All but Allison. Allison stepped off the sidewalk and listened.

Beaver-capped bears. What do I do now? Thomasina thought fast. Her argument had worked with Mother Kate and

Brother Pete. Maybe it would work here.

She tossed her head and yelled so everyone could hear, "I have as much right to march in this parade as you do, Rowdy. I don't think the people who need these donations care if they are carried by a girl or a boy. I'm not afraid of getting my boots dirty in the street."

She stared at Rowdy and then swung around to stare down Beatrice and her friends. She saw a small smile curl Allison's lips.

Rowdy said, "We'll just see about that!" He charged at Thomasina and shoved her hard. She spun around and smacked him in the chest with her package of cookies. The cookies crunched. She swung again and missed.

"You stupid, snot-nosed bully. You made me break the cookies."

Rowdy shoved his face close to her face. She could smell stale tobacco on his breath. He sneered, "It was your own doing, Miss Smarty Pants."

As Rowdy bent to jerk a piece of wood out of Zeke's saddlebags, Joe grabbed the log. He said, "Lay off, Rowdy."

Rowdy swung to face Joe. His face was as red as a miner's red underwear. He growled, "Go ahead. Take her side, you Sissy Lover."

Joe said calmly, "She's got a point, Rowdy. The people who need this wood and food won't care who brings it. Or how they get it there. Even a food-packing dog will be welcome." Joe patted Zeke on the head.

Rowdy glared at Joe, then turned and stomped off. "Well,

Zeke and the three girls fell into step. No one tried to stop them.

they ain't gonna' march close to me."

Thomasina's feeling of victory was short.

Colleen dressed in an old pair of clean overalls and holding a potato in one hand and a stick of wood in the other fell in beside Thomasina. She said, "I'll march, too."

This was not what Thomasina had planned. What could she say to stop her? She had argued that girls had the **right** to march.

Things got worse. Allison turned to her huddled friends and said, "I think she's right. I'm going to march, too."

Beatrice gasped, "You can't be serious! It isn't ladylike."

As Allison started to move away, Beatrice threatened, "If you march, don't expect to be invited to **my** Christmas party."

Allison hesitated. Then she said, "That's your choice. This is mine."

Allison walked over to Thomasina and said, "Mind if I join you?"

Thomasina was speechless. She **did** mind. Very much. This was getting out of hand. She couldn't be the first girl to march if other girls joined her. What could she do?

Joe adjusted Zeke's pack and walked off to join Rowdy and the other boys.

Thomasina thought, *Pajamaed ponies.* My big mouth has done it again.

At the head of the parade, the Grass Valley Brass Band struck up a rousing march. The front line of boys marched forward. Zeke and the three girls fell into step. No one tried to stop them.

Thomasina marched. But she was not happy.

Merchants with flour sacks and big hams joined the parade.

37

As the parade wound down Auburn Street and over Main and up Mill, rain began to fall. Merchants with flour sacks and big hams thrown over their shoulders came out of their shops and joined the parade.

Onlookers huddled under awnings over storefronts and waved. Some called out, "Hey, Thomasina. Hey, Zeke."

Thomasina plastered a smile on her wet face and waved back. The harder the rain fell, the gloomier she grew. The dirt streets turned to sticky mud.

The mud sucked off one of her boots. Thomasina jerked it out and hobbled on. This was not fun.

To make matters worse, Allison and Colleen were enjoying themselves. A few more girls skipped off the wooden sidewalks and joined the parade.

It's not fair. This was my idea. Why do they have to horn in? This was not the way it was supposed to go.

When Thomasina spied Pete in the crowd on the walkway, she threw back her head and smiled as if she were having the time of her life. She smiled until she thought her face would break.

Pete smiled, waved, and yelled, "Hey, Sis!" When he saw Allison, his hand froze in mid-air.

Thomasina's stomach flip-flopped. She felt ill.

As the parade neared *The Union* newspaper building, Allison waved at Mr. Prisk, the editor. He looked surprised when he saw the girls and Zeke. He waved and scribbled notes on his pad.

Maybe all is not lost, Thomasina thought. Maybe we'll get

our names in the newspaper. I guess that's better than nothing.

She cheered up a little. Not much.

As she slogged past the large, curved window of *The Union*, she saw a reflection. It was that figure again. It tap, tap, tapped on a rock in time with the brass band.

"Questing quizzards." What does it want? What does it mean?

The paraders were soaked and muddy when they reached the schoolhouse. Thomasina unloaded Zeke's saddlebags and ordered, "Stay." Zeke curled up near the front door. The soggy children piled their wood outside and took their other donations to their classrooms.

Trailing mud and water, Thomasina and Colleen banged through the classroom door. Thomasina said, "Red-tailed rabbits. We're in for it now. Miss Doom will nail our hides to the wall."

To her surprise, Miss Doom gave them a weak smile as they dropped their donations into the pile. She didn't mention the girl marchers.

When the class had taken their seats and settled down, Miss Doom said, "Thank you class. These donations will be most welcome to those in need."

She added, "Since most of you are wet and muddy, I won't hold you any longer. Merry Christmas. You are dismissed."

Thomasina was stunned. Didn't Miss Doom see them marching? Or was she just waiting to punish them after the holidays? Surely she didn't approve?

The children piled their wood outside and took their
other donations into the schoolhouse.

As Thomasina and Colleen rushed out the door, Colleen
looked at Thomasina closely. She said, "Thomasina you look
like you're off your feed. Has a female Tommyknocker *really*
been after you? I do believe there **could** be little people, so I
guess there **could** be female Tommyknockers . . . even though
I've never heard of such a thing."

Although Thomasina's mouth ached from keeping a fake
smile stuck on her face during the parade, she forced herself to
smile again. She said with a poor imitation of an Irish accent,
"Ah, my red-haired colleen with the milk-white skin and the
bright red speckles. Sure, and begorra, I was just a pullin' your
thin leg. And why would the wee people or a fee-male

Tommyknocker be after a'botherin' me? Are ye daft girl?"

Thomasina threw her arms into the air, tossed back her head, and shouted, "I'm fine. I'm great. A fine, great, happy, **wet**, little fee-male marcher. That's me."

Colleen nodded her cloud of red hair and said seriously, "It **was** your idea, Thomasina." Then she laughed and added, "And sure, and begorra, a princess of an idea it was. We helpless little fee-males certainly showed old Rough and Ready Rowdy a thing or two, didn't we?"

Thomasina's smile widened and deepened. "Yes," she said. "We did do that."

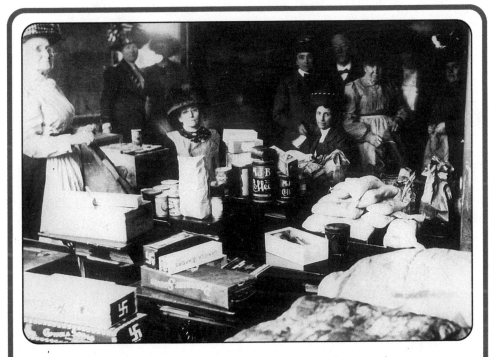

The Ladies Relief Society packed donations in boxes.

Chapter 7

Saturday was a gloomy day for Thomasina. She wasn't the "first girl to march." Fifteen girls from all the different schools had marched. Worse. No one seemed to care.

As she dragged herself to the breakfast table, Pete greeted her with a big smile. He messed her hair and asked, "How is our first female marcher this morning?"

Thomasina snapped, "Questing quizzards. Do you have to rub it in?"

Pete frowned. "Hey, Sis, I'm not rubbing it in. I'm proud of you and Zeke. And Allison and Colleen and the others," he added. His face turned pink. "Twirling toads, you girls looked great out there marching through the rain and mud. Honest."

He rubbed his nose and asked, "What's a questing quizzards?"

Thomasina tossed her head. "How should I know? I'm just your dumb little sister. Ask Smart Allison."

Kate said, "That's enough Thomasina. Pete and I are both proud of you. I don't know why you are so grumpy."

They don't understand, Thomasina thought. Everyone horned in on my idea. Pretty Allison will probably get all the credit.

Thomasina dragged her biscuit through the dark molasses

marbled with butter. She took a few bites. A lump grew in her throat. She dropped her biscuit and asked, "May I be excused?"

Mother Kate said gently, "Of course, dear."

Thomasina slouched out.

Thomasina moped in her room all day. She hated the way things had turned out. She would **never** Be Somebody.

Late in the afternoon she lay in her small bed and stared at the rain stains on her ceiling. The Tommyknocker was there. She was angry. She was pounding on a rock. Outside, the stamp mills pounded, pounded, endlessly. Thomasina thought she heard the Tommyknocker shout in time with the stamp mills, "No. No. Wrong Way. Wrong Way. Think. Think."

Kate tapped on the bedroom door.

Thomasina said, "Yes?"

Kate opened the door and said, "Sweetheart, could I ask you a favor?"

Thomasina frowned.

"I promised Mrs. Kidder I would give her a copy of a drawing I made of the Kidder mansion. She wants to show it to her guests at their big Christmas party this evening."

Thomasina sighed loudly and nodded slowly.

Grieving giraffes, she thought. Stuffy old Mrs. Kidder in her black silk dresses. I don't want to face her or Mr. Kidder's yapping, ankle-biting, little dog, Gwendolyn.

Thomasina had often heard Mr. Kidder brag how Gwendolyn would scamper up and down their long, formal dining table when it was loaded with food. But Gwendolyn would never take a bite unless Mr. Kidder ordered her to.

That must be a sight, Thomasina thought. Zeke wouldn't even fit onto our little table. And he would eat anything he found under his big nose.

What if snotty Beatrice is there? She'll only look down her nose at me.

Kate interrupted Thomasina's gloomy thoughts. "I hear the Kidders have the first Christmas tree in the county to be lighted with electric light. That must be a beautiful sight."

An electrically lighted Christmas tree. Now, **that** sounds interesting, Thomasina thought.

Thomasina sighed again. "All right, Mother."

Kate added, "Why don't you stop by the bookstore and pick up the newspaper. I'm sure it will have something on the Donation Day parade. Maybe you and Zeke will be mentioned."

Sure, Thomasina thought. Me and Smart Allison and all the other girls who joined the parade. Still, maybe, just maybe, there'll be something special about me . . . and Zeke.

Thomasina dragged herself off the bed and called Zeke.

By the time Thomasina and Zeke reached the Grass Valley railroad depot, it was dusk. As they trudged toward the Kidder mansion across from the depot, Thomasina stopped in amazement. Colored lights—red, green, white, and blue—flooded out the large front windows. They were beautiful.

So those are electric Christmas lights, she thought—a-maa-zzing!

Thomasina stood for some time watching the colors dance out the windows. Then she slowly thumped up the steps to the mansion. She rang the bell. It clang, clanged inside. Gwendolyn yapped in a nervous, high-pitched bark. Zeke answered with a deep, vibrant "Woof!" The stamp mills pounded, pounded. Thomasina's heart thudded.

Beatrice opened the door.

Thomasina shuffled her feet and jerked at her stockings. *Grumpy geese.* Just my luck.

Beatrice looked down her nose and said coolly, "May I help you Miss Thomasina?"

For a minute Thomasina couldn't speak.

Beatrice asked impatiently, "May I help you?"

Thomasina held out the drawing and stammered, "Uh . . . Ah . . . oh. Th . . . this is for Mrs. Kidder." Thomasina felt her face flush. Why do Beatrice and her mansion make me feel so small and unimportant?

Beatrice took the drawing and ordered, "Wait here." She closed the door.

Thomasina shivered and patted Zeke on the head. She tiptoed over to the big windows and peeked in.

She drew in a deep breath. This must be the most beautiful Christmas tree in the Whole Wide World.

The tree was strung with red, green, blue, and white electric lights and covered with delicate glass ornaments in all sizes and shapes. It was draped with golden ropes and topped with a

Colored light flooded out the large front window.

beautiful angel in a flowing white silk gown.

Oh, if only I could have a tree like that. It must have cost a fortune. Where did they get the tree and the decorations? I've never seen anything like them in my whole life.

And electric lights on a Christmas tree!

As Thomasina gazed in wonder, the large door opened a crack. Beatrice shoved out the big blue ribbon she had worn on Donation Day. Gwendolyn peeked between Beatrice's shiny, high-topped boots and yapped.

Beatrice said, "Here. This color does not suit me. You may have it in payment for the drawing."

Thomasina's felt the blood drain from her face. She wanted to throw the limp ribbon in Beatrice's sassy face. She wanted to tell her to tie it on fancy, spoiled Gwendolyn. But Thomasina could see that Gwendolyn already had a pretty pink bow tied in her white, stringy hair. The bow matched her pink dog collar.

Zeke turned his back and stared silently at the bright moon. Thomasina clamped her teeth together to keep the angry words from pouring out. She stared icily at Beatrice, took the ribbon, and said, "Thank you."

Thomasina turned and stumbled down the stairs. At the bottom she stopped and hugged Zeke. Salty tears splashed down her face. Why is life so unfair? Why should snotty Beatrice have everything?

Zeke wagged his tail and licked her tears as if to tell her he didn't know.

Chapter 8

Thomasina turned to take one last look at the most beautiful Christmas tree in the world.

"Come on, Zeke. Let's go pick up the newspaper. It's getting darker."

Thomasina wasn't afraid of the dark. Zeke was with her. The full moon that peeked through the pine trees was so bright she could see her shadow.

Thomasina and Zeke ran to the nearest bookstore. Thomasina slapped down two pennies and grabbed the evening paper.

There it was. All about Donation Day on the third page. Thomasina's shoulders sagged lower and lower as she read: "This year, for the first time, several girls marched in the parade." That was all. No names.

Cross-eyed cows.

On the same page, a long article described the elegant Christmas party planned by the Kidders. It went on and on about "the social event of the season." A Christmas tree imported from Boston. Hand-blown glass ornaments imported from Europe. Electric Christmas tree lights—the first in the county—imported from New York. Delicate cakes and sweetmeats for the guests. All shipped in from San Francisco on Kidder's little railroad.

Thomasina couldn't breathe. She felt like Rowdy had slammed into her again. Her plan to Be Somebody had failed. Now this! The long list of guests included all the rich and well-know people in the county. Mine owners, judges, government officials, doctors, merchants, newspaper editors, bankers, and investors. Mr. Kidder was to send a special train to Colfax to meet important guests coming in on the Southern Pacific train from Sacramento and San Francisco.

Allison Coleman wasn't on the list.

Thomasina smirked. Guess Beatrice kept her threat. Serves Allison right for poking her nose where it wasn't wanted.

Thomasina started to tear the paper to shreds. She stopped. Mother and Pete would want to read it.

We're not the Kidders. We can't throw away even two pennies. We could **never** afford a beautiful Christmas tree or a big party. Why is life so unfair? I'll never Be Somebody because we don't have a lot of money.

Thomasina folded the newspaper and called, "Zeke, let's go home."

As Thomasina slumped past the old abandoned mine shaft near her home, she heard a loud tap, tap, tapping.

Zeke laid his ears back and whined.

The pounding grew louder. Someone shouted, "Cross-eyed cows!"

Thomasina jumped. Who could that be? Someone is playing our crazy critters game.

Thomasina peeked over a large rock. There was the

figment of her imagination. A tiny female.

"Thomasina Starr," the figure shouted, "I'm warning you. You are going too far."

Thomasina gasped.

The tiny female hammered harder and harder with each word. "Don't just stand there looking at me with those big cow-eyes." *Bang!* "Sit down and listen." *Bang!* "Listen hard." *Bang!*

"I'm warning you. You are in trouble!" *Bang!*

Thomasina plopped down on a large rock. She stared open-mouthed at the tiny female.

She's loud and mad, Thomasina thought, but she's small. She can't do me much harm.

Thomasina could see the figure clearly in the moonlight. She was about one-foot tall. She was old. Her face was not pretty, but not ugly. It was wrinkled. Her long, straggly gray hair streamed off in all directions. A few black strands peeped through the gray. A sprig of manzanita dangled near her right ear. Her brown eyes sparkled beneath dark bushy eyebrows. Her nose was large. Her pink lips were full. Her fat cheeks, as red as ripe strawberries.

A green velvet cloak hung from her shoulders to the top of her heavy work boots. A small strap of tan animal skin wound around her neck. Bright red, green, and blue ribbons and scarves dangled here and there. A brilliant blue pheasant feather fluttered down her left sleeve. A red braided cord swung a leather tool holder from her waist. All in all, she was a most colorful sight.

Thomasina peeked over a large rock and saw a tiny female with a tiny miner's pick in her hand.

Thomasina wondered, Is she really a female Tommy-knocker? As if she had read Thomasina's mind, the figure snapped. "Of course I'm a female Tommyknocker, you ninny. You can call me Winny. I'm here to help you . . . . If there **is** any help for you."

Thomasina thought, I've never **heard** of a female Tommy-knocker.

Winny jumped about as if she were dancing on hot coals. She fussed with her colorful ribbons and tried to smooth her fly-away hair.

She smacked her tiny pick against the rock, and shouted, "Grieving garter snakes. If there are male Tommyknockers, there are female Tommyknockers. That stands to reason. Ask any male Tommyknocker you see. Females just don't get much credit for what they do."

Thomasina's tongue came unglued. "What do they do?"

"We do what male Tommyknockers do. We warn people when they're in trouble. That's why I'm here."

Winny fiddled with a strand of hair and harrumphed, "For your information, I'm one foot and three inches tall. I have my mother's nose. It **is** large. Sign of strength and character. But, I'm **not** old. I'm only 322, to be exact. I'm not even married yet."

"You're 322 years old and not married?" Thomasina blurted.

"Jumping June bugs, girl. Do I have to repeat everything? Of course I'm not married. I lived with my parents until I was 101 years 3 months and 2 days old. Tommyknockers don't marry until we're at least 400. By that age we have enough sense to tell gold from fool's gold. Then we can pick a good mate. That's your problem. You can't see real gold when it's right under your nose."

Thomasina shouted back, "I can so. I could tell the difference between fool's gold and real gold when I was six."

Winny stomped her foot. "Then you'd better go back to being six. Besides, I'm not talking about mineral gold. I'm talking about the gold in your creative imagination. The gold in people's hearts. The gold of good friends. **You** can't see a friend through a barbed-wire fence."

Thomasina squirmed. "Wha . . ."

Winny ordered. "Don't interrupt."

She continued in a rush. "Lately you've been acting like a foolish adult. All that is important to them is 'What does it cost? Who is the prettiest? Who has the fastest horses and the fanciest carriages? Who wears the biggest bustle? Who has the most jammed-crammed parlor?' Which they **never** sit in.

"I'm warning you. You are missing the real gold. You'd better wake up before you suffer permanent adult-thinking damage. Wake up, now!"

Bang! Bang! Bang! Winny smacked the tiny pick against the rock.

Thomasina jumped. "Well, you don't have to bite my head off."

Winny harrumphed and folded her arms across her chest. "I've a mind to. But you need your head . . . and, you'd better learn to use it."

Thomasina said, "I . . . I thought Tommyknockers only appeared in mines to warn miners of danger."

Winny shrugged. "Simple mistake. Mines and minds. We do live in mines. But we can appear anywhere to people who have the magical imagination needed to see and hear us."

Thomasina asked, "Are you real or are you only in my imagination?"

Winny kicked her boot against a rock. "Zeroed zebras. Do you **believe** I'm real?"

Thomasina paused. "Yes. Yes, I do."

"Then I **am** real. I am real as long as you imagine me."

"That's hard to understand," Thomasina said. "Why am I the only one who sees you?"

"Because you have a healthy, active imagination.

Winny.

Part of you knows you're being a fool. Part of you wants to wake up and find the real gold!"

Winny smacked the pick against the rock. *Bang, bang, bang!* She jumped about wildly and cried, "Warning. Warning. Danger. Danger."

Thomasina shouted, "Bellowing birdies. I am awake!

Where am I in trouble? Where and what is all this gold I can't see?"

Winny jammed the pick into its holder. She took a deep breath and jabbed her finger at Thomasina. "Here's where you're in trouble. You don't see the real gold in Joe and Allison, and—even Miss Doom."

"Bu . . ."

"Rude reindeers! Don't interrupt. And Chief Wema, Irish Jim, and many of the people you know. Your mother sees the real gold in these people. That's why she draws them. You think they're not important because you have known them all your life. They're in your own backyard.

"Slobbering snakes. You are right to think of them as 'just people.' They are. But they are a rich and rare mixture of races and cultures."

Winny pulled at her hair and swung her arms wildly. "Feathered frogs. Look around you, girl! The people and this place are more colorful and rare than any poke of gold or set of colored electric lights on a tree."

Winny plopped down on a rock and wiped her sweaty face with her sleeve. She said slowly and calmly, "Think with your brain. See with your imagination. Listen with your heart."

"Bu . . ."

Winny snapped, "Don't interrupt. It's rude, and I'm not finished."

"You interrupted me—twice," Thomasina whined.

"Well," Winny said, "I'm young. I still have a few faults.

Besides, you imagine me this way."

Winny rushed on. "One last point. You marched in the parade for the wrong reason."

Thomasina jumped to her feet and stuck her chin out. She towered over Winny. "If you please, Miss Winny, I marched to help the needy."

"Stuff and nonsense, Thomasina. You, I, and Zeke know the reason. You **did** want to help the needy. That was right. But the real reason you marched was to get your name in the newspaper so you could Be Somebody."

"What's wrong with that?" Thomasina snapped.

"Nothing, really, if you do the right thing and for the right reasons."

"It **was** my idea," Thomasina grumped.

"Yes, and it was a good idea," Winny agreed. "But you should be happy that other girls joined in. But, no. Not you. You wanted to hog all the glory for yourself!) The point is, girls **should** march."

Winny jumped up and pointed at the newspaper laying at Thomasina's feet. "If today's headlines had blared THOMASINA STARR, FIRST GIRL TO MARCH IN THE DONATION DAY PARADE, would you Be Somebody?"

"Yes!" Thomasina shouted.

Winny put her hands on her hips and looked up into Thomasina's eyes. "Yes . . . perhaps . . . for a day or two. One hundred years from now hardly anyone will know or care when the first girls marched or who they were. Just as people don't know who built the first fire or made the first biscuit."

Winny rubbed her chin thoughtfully. "Personally, I think fire and biscuits are more important. Still, you and the other girls did a good thing."

"But you're supposed to help me," Thomasina whined. "You know what I want. How can I get to Be Somebody?"

Winny patted her flying hair and said, "I can't tell you anything you don't already know or can't figure out for yourself. I'm just here to warn you. You're prospecting a false lead. You're looking in the wrong places."

"You're a big help," Thomasina snapped.

Winny barked, "I can't lay the answer in your lap."

Zeke slid down on his belly, shut his eyes, and hid his head under his paws as if the argument was hurting his ears.

Winny lowered her voice and touched Thomasina's hand. "Tell me, girl, do you think Beatrice gets everything she wants?"

Thomasina plopped down on a rock. She picked up the crumpled newspaper and Beatrice's blue ribbon. She looked at the expensive ribbon and then down at her old, muddy boots. She tugged at her wet stockings.

"I can't think of anything she could want that she **doesn't** have. She's rich. She's plump and pretty. She lives in a mansion. She has the most beautiful Christmas tree in the world. All the important people in the county are going to the Kidders' big, fancy party."

Winny's hair billowed in the breeze as she stomped in circles. "Questing quizzards, girl. You don't need money for a beautiful Christmas tree or a grand party. You make me so

57

hopping mad. The answer is right under your nose. Use your imagination. Look for the real gold."

Thomasina stared dumbfounded.

Winny jerked out her tiny pick. She pulled at her hair, tugged at her ribbons, hammered with her pick, and stomped her feet. Bang, bang, bang! The pounding grew louder and louder.

Zeke opened his eyes. He slowly lifted himself onto his front feet, raised his big head, and gave a long rising howl.

Thomasina yelled over the noise, "Look where?"

With a BANG louder than a dynamite blast, Winny disappeared in a brilliant light.

Zeke stopped in mid-howl.

Thomasina blinked. "Wow! Did I **really** see and hear all that? Have the moonlight and my imagination played a trick on me? My eyes hurt and my ears ring. That's real enough.

If the answer is under my nose, what is it?

Thomasina looked down. All she saw was the crumpled newspaper and Beatrice's big blue ribbon in her lap.

Thomasina looked around slowly. "Zeke, Old Boy, did you hear and see that?"

Zeke wagged his tail.

Chapter 9

Thomasina started home in a daze. "What was Winny trying to tell me?" From between the pine trees, the dim lights from their cabin looked warm and inviting. The closer she and Zeke got, the faster they ran. They burst through the door letting in a cold draft of night air.

Mother Kate was sitting in front of the fireplace.

She looked up from her book. "Here's my merry girl. I was getting worried. Did you deliver the Kidders' drawing?"

Thomasina blurted, "Yes, Mother I did and, Mother, I saw a Tom . . . ." Thomasina bit off her words in midstream. Would Mother Kate believe she had seen a female Tommyknocker? She wasn't sure she even believed it.

Mother Kate said patiently, "You met Tom who?"

"Uh . . . Oh . . . I met this new girl, Winny, who is a . . . is a . . . tom . . . tomboy, just like me."

Thomasina quickly changed the subject. "And I saw the Kidders' tree. Mother, it is the most beautiful tree I have ever seen. It sits in the big front windows of the Kidder mansion and the colored electric lights pour out onto the lawn. It's like something out of a fairy tale. So beautiful. So colorful."

Thomasina's excitement dribbled away. She handed Mother Kate the paper.

59

"Here, you can read all about it in the paper."

"Is there anything about Donation Day?"

Thomasina flopped into a chair. "Oh, they mention that some girls marched for the first time. No names."

Kate said softly, "I'm sorry, dear. I thought they might mention you and Zeke. You must have made a striking pair. But the newspaper can't cover everything."

Thomasina crossed her arms over her chest and har-rumphed, "Well, they certainly told all about the Kidders' Christmas tree and party."

Thomasina held up the big blue ribbon. "That reminds me. Beatrice gave me this ribbon in payment for your drawing of the mansion. Said the color didn't suit her."

Mother Kate laughed softly and shook her head. "I've received some rare and beautiful gifts for my drawings, but this is most unusual. Instead of handmade, it's hand-me-down."

She smiled at Thomasina. "Never mind. Hand-me-downs are as good as gold if you need them. It hardly goes with any of your dresses, does it dear?"

Thomasina frowned. "No, it doesn't."

Kate said, "I'm sure with your clever mind you will find a use for it."

Kate got up and kneeled before Thomasina.

"My precious girl. I do so wish I could give you frilly dresses and fancy parties and electric lights on Christmas trees. But I can't."

Thomasina's chest tightened. She didn't want to make her mother unhappy.

She forced a smile and said, "Oh, Mother, Beatrice doesn't have everything. She doesn't have you, or Pete, or Zeke. We'll have a happy Christmas. Just you wait and see."

Kate swiped at her eyes and said, "That's my girl. We can't afford an expensive tree. Only a few families have trees. But, we can enjoy the big church Christmas tree tomorrow. I hear that Cornish Lou is being her usual generous self.

"A great pile of gifts arrived at the local churches a few days ago. They were all gaily wrapped. Every child under the age of fourteen who goes to church tomorrow will find a gift under their church's community tree."

Thomasina blurted, "Why does Cornish Lou do it? All the ladies in town turn up their noses when they see her on the streets. They would never invite her into their homes. If I had money, I wouldn't buy presents for children of people who didn't like me."

Kate was annoyed. "Good gracious, Thomasina, you need to work on your Christmas spirit. Cornish Lou doesn't buy the presents to make people like her. I'm sure she does it because she enjoys doing it. It must make her happy to make the children happy. I can understand that. Can't you?"

Thomasina shrugged. She knew that Cornish Lou never admitted she sent the presents year after year. But all the shopkeepers knew who bought them. Word gets around in a small town.

Kate continued. "Cornish Lou may not be a proper lady, but each Christmas she is an unnamed angel to the local children. I respect her for that. Some children would get no presents at all if it were not for Cornish Lou."

Kate pointed her finger at Thomasina. "Count your blessings. We have a roof over our heads, a fire in the stove, food on the table, and each other. That's much more than many have."

That was one of the longest lectures Thomasina had ever heard from her mother.

Thomasina blurted, "Oh, Mother, I know. But, bow-legged bullfrogs, I want so much more."

"So do I, dear heart. So do I."

Kate started toward the kitchen. "How about a cup of hot apple cider and then to bed?"

"A cup of warm cider sounds good. But I don't think I'll sleep much tonight."

"My merry girl, I think you will. You've had a busy day. And Zeke, too. Let's give him a special treat."

Thomasina smiled. "Can we let Zeke eat off our fine china at the formal dining table?"

Mother Kate laughed. "Dancing dodo birds. Don't play Mr. Kidder with me. Zeke will eat from his old bowl on the floor. Zeke's too smart to be a snob."

Later, as Thomasina lay in bed staring out the window at the starry night, her head buzzed with questions. What was Winny trying to tell me? Will I **ever** Be Somebody?

Mother Kate was right. Thomasina no sooner uncurled her feet inch by inch to warm up the cold sheets than she fell into a deep sleep.

She dreamed.

Familiar faces and sounds danced and banged through her head. She and Zeke slogged through mud and rain. Zeke's bells jingled.

Winny hammered. Softly at first. *Knock. Knock. Knock.* Then louder. *Bang. Bang. Bang!*

Beatrice's blue ribbon and a red feather floated into a tree.

The faces on Mother Kate's drawings danced round and round as Old Zeb droned, "You bet. You bet."

Allison waved. Brother Pete smiled. Joe wiped his nose on his sleeve and grinned. Colleen held up a potato. Miss Doom smiled weakly and nodded.

Thomas Starr's photograph waltzed with bunches of dried flowers and white lace. Mother Kate's handmade gifts and gingerbread cookies swung and swayed from bright ribbons.

Thomasina tossed and turned.

Winny stomped her boots and banged with her tiny miner's pick. She shrieked, "Under your nose!"

A loud "Bang!" A shrill "Shriek!"

Thomasina popped upright in bed. "What was that?"

Then she knew. It was a mine whistle blowing the change of shift. In the distance, the stamp mills thud, thudded. Thomasina's heart pounded.

I can't make heads or tails of this, she thought. Flowers and faces. Mother's gifts and ribbons. White lace, a red feather, and Beatrice's blue bow. What does it mean?

Thomasina pulled her knees up and sat with her chin cupped in her hands. She thought hard as she looked out the window. The dawn light painted the fluffy clouds pink. The small grove of young fir trees behind the garden sparkled with frost jewels. There on the tip top of a small fir tree Winny smiled and made a sawing motion with her tiny pick.

Pow! The idea came in a blaze as sudden and bright as when Winny disappeared with a bang.

Thomasina knew what to do.

Winny was on the tip top of a small fir tree.

Chapter 10

Thomasina heard Mother Kate stirring the fire in the kitchen stove. Zeke pushed opened the bedroom door and padded to her bed. Thomasina grabbed him by his big ears and whispered, "This time I think I've got it right!"

A few minutes later Zeke and Thomasina slammed into the kitchen.

Thomasina hugged Mother Kate and danced away chanting, "I think I've got it! Got it. Got it."

"Have what?" Kate asked.

"What Winny was trying to tell me."

"Who is Winny?"

"Why, Winny is a Tomm . . . ." Thomasina stopped. "Oh, remember? Winny is the tomboy I met the other day after the Donation Day parade. She's different from anyone I ever met. She jumps around and fidgets. A fidgety-gibberty. She's kind of loud and talks a lot."

Mother Kate looked at Thomasina and then into the distance. "She sounds like someone I know very well."

Mother Kate was silent for a second. Then she added, "After church this morning, I'm going to take the little train to Chicago Park. I want to do some drawings. I'll probably stop and chat with Mrs. Sonntag and pick up some jugs of apple cider that she has been saving for me.

"I'll get back to Grass Valley in time to hear the miners' Cornish Choir sing in front of the Holbrooke Hotel. I hope you don't mind my leaving you alone most of the day. Maybe you could visit with your new friend Winny. It sounds like the two of you have a lot in common."

Thomasina jigged up and down and twisted a piece of her hair. "What's Pete doing today?"

"Oh, he was off first thing this morning. After church he's going to visit with his friends who are home for the holidays. They will probably get up a football game at Glenbrook Park in the afternoon."

Bow-tied buffaloes, Thomasina thought. Things couldn't be better. I'll have the house to myself almost all day.

Later at church, Thomasina pushed her way to the front row to see the community Christmas tree. It was nice, but not nearly as beautiful as the Kidders'. And nothing like the vision she now carried in her imagination.

After the services, she rushed to be one of the first in line to receive her present. She knew she was being rude, but she had important things to do.

As she waited, she shuffled her feet, tugged at her stockings, and waved to Joe and Colleen farther back in the line. At soon as she was handed her present, Thomasina hurried out of church. She didn't stop to chat with Colleen. She didn't open the present. She didn't even stop to rattle a stick along the Coleman's iron fence.

She ran past the Kidder mansion. The tree in the window wasn't as magical as it had been at night with its colored dancing lights.

As soon as she got home, Thomasina rummaged around in the tool shed. "Here it is, Zeke. A saw. Let's go play Paul Bunyan."

Thomasina finished just at sunset. She stoked up the kitchen stove, put another log into the fireplace, and lighted four kerosene lanterns. Then she stood back to admire her work.

"Well, Zeke, what do you think? Is that something? I did it all with my imagination—and a lot of prodding from Winny. How do you like it?"

Zeke raised his right paw and wagged his tail.

"Good Old Zeke. You are easy to please. I hope Mother and Pete like what I did with what I found right under my nose."

Thomasina jumped when the door suddenly opened letting in a cold blast of air. Thomasina smiled. It was Pete.

"Hi, Big Brother," she called.

"Greetings, Little Sis," he said. "Where's Mother? I thought she would be home by now." A shadowed figure stood in the half-open door. "I have someone I want her to meet. I think you already know her."

Before Thomasina could answer, Pete turned and led the figure into the lamplight.

Snotgurgles. It was Allison! How could Pete do this to me?

allison B.

"Wow! Where did the beautiful Christmas
tree come from?"

My surprise tree was just for him and Mother. Does Allison have to spoil everything again?

Thomasina clenched her fists and tightened her jaw.

Before she could say anything, Pete and Allison noticed the tree. They both gasped.

Pete said, "Wow! Where did the beautiful Christmas tree come from?"

As Allison walked closer to the tree she said, "It's beautiful. Beautiful. This is the most beautiful and original tree I have ever seen. Who did it? Thomasina, was it you?"

Thomasina bit her tongue. Why does everything go wrong for me? Allison is just being nice because she likes Pete. I hate her. Thomasina said coolly, "I didn't do it."

"Then who did, Little Sis?"

Thomasina snapped, "Don't call me Little Sis. You're just making fun of me."

Pete's smile faded. "Honest, Thomasina I'm not. That is some tree. I've never seen one like it. If you did it, you should be proud. Yes, sireee. That is some tree." He tried to mess Thomasina's hair, but she jerked away.

Allison said, "Truly, Thomasina. This is the most beautiful Christmas tree I have even seen."

For spite, Thomasina asked, "More beautiful than the Kidders' tree?" She knew Allison hadn't been invited to the Kidders' party.

Allison said with a light laugh, "Well, I really don't know about that. I haven't seen the Kidders' Christmas tree. Beatrice didn't invite me after I muddied my boots to march in the

69

Donation Day parade."

Thomasina smirked. She thought Old Pokey-Nose Allison was getting just what she deserved.

Pete said, "Thomasina, if you didn't do the Christmas tree, who did?"

Without thinking Thomasina blurted, "Winny . . . Winny, the Tommyknocker."

Pete threw back his head and laughed, long and loud. "You little Cornish imp. You would think up something like that. Come on. You did the tree, didn't you?"

Before Thomasina could answer, the door opened. The kerosene lamps fluttered and the fire in the fireplace flared. Mother Kate pushed through the door carrying her drawing pad and two jugs of apple cider.

She said, "Hello, dears," and stopped short. She looked at the tree and drew in a long breath. Her eyes widened as she looked from Pete to Allison to Thomasina.

"It's beautiful. A beautiful Christmas tree. Decorated with our handmade gifts, and my drawings, and flowers and ribbons and lace. And topped with Thomas' photograph. How lovely. How thoughtful." Tears of happiness sparkled in her eyes.

Again she looked from Pete to Allison to Thomasina. "Who did this wonderful tree?"

Pete laughed and said, "Thomasina says Winny the Tommyknocker did it."

Mother Kate smiled a secret smile at Thomasina and said, "You know I met a Tommyknocker once." Kate looked into the distance. "She reminded me of someone I knew."

Thomasina jigged with delight. "Did she talk a lot, ask a lot of questions, jump around, and make lots of noise?"

"Yes. Yes, indeed she did, Thomasina. How wonderful that Winny did this lovely tree for us."

Thomasina stammered, "Uh . . . well . . .Winny didn't really do . . . . but she . . . . and, well . . . I thought . . . ." Thomasina bit her tongue and stopped.

Mother Kate filled the silence. "Well, here I stand with my two jugs of apple cider. The beauty of the tree made me forget my manners." She set down the jugs, turned to Allison, and said, "I don't think I have had the pleasure."

Pete blushed and said, "Mother I would like you to meet Allison Coleman." He added with a rush, "Allison and I were talking about your drawings after the football game. She wanted to meet you."

Allison stepped forward to shake Kate's offered hand. "Yes, Mrs. Starr I have long admired your art. I have seen your drawings in New York magazines. I am honored to meet you. It isn't often that a woman builds up the reputation you have as an artist."

Kate said, "Thank you."

Pink-tailed panthers, Thomasina thought. Pokey Nose spreads flattery around like she was buttering a biscuit with Old Betsy's butter.

Kate picked up the jugs and headed toward the kitchen. "Shall we all have some hot cider and enjoy the warm fire and Thoma . . . and Winny's . . . lovely tree?"

Chapter 11

The little group sat in front of the fireplace drinking hot apple cider. Allison couldn't take her eyes off the tree—except when she glanced at Pete. When their eyes met, Pete's face blazed and his eyes turned soft and dreamy.

Questing quizzards. Thomasina thought. I hope I never get as cow-eyed as those two. But they do seem to like the tree.

Allison asked, "Where did all these marvelous decorations come from?"

Thomasina smiled and said nothing.

Mother Kate explained, "Some are gifts from people who posed for me."

Allison added, "I recognize many of the faces in the drawings." She pointed them out. "There's Irish Jim, Juan Juarez, Old Zeb, Cornish Lou, and Mrs. Sonntag. This is a wonderful drawing of the Kidder mansion."

Thomasina couldn't stay quiet any longer. "The Indian basket was made by Chief Wema's wife. Juan Juarez made the donkey piñata. Ah Ling decorated the egg with Chinese symbols of good luck."

Thomasina couldn't cork her happiness. It bubbled over. She jumped up and moved from decoration to decoration.

She babbled happily. "The ribbons and lace came from

Miss Wren, the dressmaker. Mother made the gingerbread cookies. Cornish Lou gave me the red ostrich feather. I . . . we . . . didn't have an angel for the top of the tree. So we stuck Beatrice Kidder's big blue bow behind my father's photograph and placed it at the top of the tree."

Everyone gave Thomasina their full attention.

She rushed on, "The dried flowers came from Mother's studio. Mother and I grew them in the garden last summer."

Pete interrupted, "Where did Winny get the tree?"

Thomasina explained, "It's a small fir from behind the garden."

Thomasina told them where each decoration came from.

"Bow-legged bunnies. You sure know a lot about what Winny did, Thomasina."

"Winny **is** very clever," Kate added with a knowing look.

Allison said, "Yes, she is clever." She turned to Pete. "Everyone should see this tree. We should have a big party so everyone can come and see what Thoma . . . I mean, Winny the Tommyknocker *and* Thomasina have done with their gifts."

Thomasina smiled. Allison is a butt-in-ski, she thought, but a party would be fun.

As the little group sat long into the night chatting about the tree, they planned a party. They would invite Juan Juarez, Old Zeb, Cornish Lou, and Chief Wema and his wife. They would invite everyone who was in any way a part of the Christmas tree.

It would be a simple party. Everyone would be asked to bring whatever food and drink they could.

Thomasina chimed in, "Sort of like the Donation Day parade. If everyone brings one dish, it will build up to a big feast." She added with a laugh, "Even one small potato will help."

Chapter 12

The next two days, Thomasina helped Mother Kate made dozens of saffron buns and piles of Cornish pasties.

She noticed that Mother Kate and Allison held several secret meetings. When Mother Kate wasn't cooking, she spent a lot of time in her studio with the door locked. Thomasina was curious as to what Allison and Mother Kate were up to, but she knew better than to ask too many questions. She didn't want to spoil any special Christmas secrets.

On Friday, the day before the party, Thomasina, in a cheerful holiday spirit, offered to pick up the evening paper. Mother Kate jumped as if Thomasina had offered to bring home an angry hive of bees. Kate patted her hair, fiddled with her apron, and said, "Oh, oh, no. Thank you, Thomasina. Allison and Pete will pick up the newspaper on their way home from the errands they are running."

Thomasina knew something was being kept from her, but she let it go. She had too much holiday spirit to spoil anyone's fun with a pokey nose.

The next day, on Saturday afternoon, people began to arrive.

Chief Wema and his wife carried in a large pot of fragrant acorn soup.

Juan Juarez brought a high stack of tortillas and a pot of beans.

Mrs. Sonntag and two of her children carried in four golden brown apple pies.

Cornish Lou lugged in sacks and sacks of goodies from Foley's Candy Store.

Miss Wren brought in a box of Felix Gillet's famous French dessert prunes.

Irish Jim lugged in a pot of corned beef and cabbage. He bowed and kissed the ladies and twirled Thomasina around the kitchen in a wild Irish jig.

Miss Doom unveiled a big, rich chocolate cake.

Old Zeb hung a sprig of mistletoe over the kitchen door. "A good bet. Yeap, you bet," he said as nodded his head.

The table didn't actually groan with the heavy load of food, but people did as they eyed the feast and smacked their lips.

Joe and Colleen came in together.

Colleen's dress was plain but new. Her wild red hair was pulled back and corralled by a bright green ribbon. A few wispy curls strayed out around her ears and forehead. As she handed Thomasina a plate of sugar cookies, she shrugged her shoulders. She said, "Mother made me make them. They may not be fit for the hogs."

"Slobbering snakes," Thomasina whispered. "You cooked! You actually cooked. And your dress and hair are stunn-ning, ab-so-lu-tely stunn-ning!"

76

People poured in and out of the cabin in a warm happy stream. Everyone added a dish to the table.

Colleen smiled and said, "Don't rub it in, Big Mouth."

Joe's red hair was parted in the middle and firmly plastered down. His blue eyes sparkled in the midst of his shiny freckled face. He blushed as he shyly handed Thomasina a softball that was used, but in fair condition. He wiped his nose on the frayed sleeve of his boiled white shirt. He hung his head and said, "You can't eat it. But I thought you and Colleen could use it."

"Oh, Joe. We certainly can. Our old ball is only held together with spit and imagination."

She added, "And I have a little something for you."

Thomasina rushed to the tree and pulled out a small, soft

package. She handed it to Joe. "Now, don't take this wrong."

Joe opened the package. It was two large white handkerchiefs.

Joe laughed. "Why thank you, Tom, Tom. Guess you can't call me snot nose now."

Thomasina said, "Well, I can. But I'll **try** not to."

People poured in and out of the cabin in a warm, happy stream. Everyone added a dish to the table. Everyone admired the tree. Each person stared longest at the drawing of their own face and their own handmade gift. But they politely admired the other drawings and decorations.

Allison and Kate stayed busy serving hot apple cider and telling everyone to "Help yourself."

Everyone did.

Pete was everywhere—shaking hands, stirring the fire, and tossing coats into a big pile on Thomasina's bed.

Zeke lifted his right paw, wagged his tail, and smiled at everyone until he received his pat on the head.

Thomasina talked more than she had ever talked in her life—which was **a lot**. She explained to each person, over and over, how Winny the Tommyknocker had helped her decorate the tree.

Some wanted to hear and re-hear all about the female Tommyknocker. Others only nodded and smiled.

The party went on for three hours. Thomasina was hopping with happiness.

When the cider jugs were dry and the groaning table of food was reduced to a whisper of crumbs, the last few stragglers said their "Thanks" and "Merry Christmases."

Cornish Lou, the last guest—and the loudest and most talkative next to Thomasina—finally talked her way out the door. Kate shut the door softly and sighed. "What a pleasant party, and such interesting and good-hearted people."

Kate gave Thomasina a hard hug, and said, "My merry girl. I am most proud of you."

"Why? What did I do?"

"You were a gracious hostess. You made everyone feel welcome and important."

"Well . . ." Thomasina said slowly, "they are important. Without them there would have been no decorations for the tree. They deserve all the credit. And, Winny, of course, for pounding the idea into my head."

"Of course," Kate said.

Thomasina couldn't hold in her happiness. She spun in circles with open arms. She wanted to hug the whole world. She stopped in front of the tree and shouted, "Winny, that was the most elegant, swell-elegant party ever. Too bad, you didn't show up to see how much everyone enjoyed **our** tree."

Mother Kate gasped, "Oh! Thomasina, in all the excitement I forget to tell you."

"Forgot to tell me what?"

"Winny was here earlier and she left you something."

"Questing quizzards. What? Where?"

Mother Kate said, "Just a minute."

She called toward the kitchen, "Pete and Allison, please come and join us."

"Be right there, Mother."

Thomasina tugged at her hair and jigged on one foot. What could it be?

Zeke padded in and flopped at Thomasina's feet.

Pete stood in the kitchen door wearing an apron and wiping his hands on a dish cloth. Allison peeked over Pete's shoulder. The hot tub of dish water had reddened her cheeks and loosened wisps of blond curls around her face.

To her amazement, Thomasina saw that Allison was rather pretty.

Kate stooped under the Christmas tree and drew out a small square package. It was wrapped in purple paper and tied with a bright red bow.

Kate handed Thomasina the present. "Winny left this for you."

"Ohhh . . ."

Thomasina tore off the ribbon and ripped off the paper. She held a small book.

She looked up at Kate, then at Pete, then at Allison. They were smiling. Pete poked Allison lightly in the ribs and she giggled.

Pete said, "Open it, Little Sis . . . . I mean . . . open it, Thomasina." Thomasina opened the cover carefully.

To Somebody Named Thomasina

was written inside in a tiny, clear handwriting.

The first page was a colored drawing of their Christmas tree. The next page was an article cut from Friday's *Union* newspaper.

The article told all about the Christmas tree in Mrs. Thomas Starr's living room that had been decorated by Thomasina Starr and Winny, a local female Tommyknocker. At the end, the article listed the people who had been invited to attend a Christmas party at the Starr's cabin on the twenty-fourth of December, 1892 to celebrate the first Tommyknocker Christmas tree in Nevada County, California.

The article was signed, "Allison Coleman, A Female Scribbler."

Thomasina's eyes sparkled as she read each word.

She carefully turned the other pages. Each page was a small drawing by Mother Kate of the people who were at the party—including Zeke.

On the last page, in tiny handwriting, Thomasina read:

*P.S. You **do** know the difference between gold and fool's gold! Stay out of trouble!!*
                              Winny, The Tommyknocker

At the bottom right-hand corner was a drawing of a tiny miner's pick.

A Note from the Author
About Grass Valley, California

Grass Valley, California was one of the largest gold mining camps in California during the gold rush of 1848 and 1849. By 1852, the gold rush was over. The easily found placer gold had been picked out of most of the streams of Northern California. Most of the miners, who had come to the California gold fields from throughout the world, returned to their homes. Hundreds of gold mining camps disappeared. Grass Valley did not.

Grass Valley continued to grow when deposits of gold-rich quartz rock that reached thousands of feet underground were discovered.

Hundreds of mine shafts and tunnels were dug deep into the earth so chunks of gold-quartz could be pounded off mine walls. Mules that spent their entire lives underground pulled ore carts filled with these large rocks to hoisting machines where the rocks, called ore, were pulled to the surface. Hundreds of large metal stamp mills ran twenty-four hours a day, seven days a week, pounding these large rocks into smaller rocks. After the gold was separated from this crushed ore by chemicals, the pure gold was melted and poured into gold bars called bullion.

In 1892—when Thomasina Starr met Winny, a female Tommyknocker—Grass Valley was one of the largest and